Who Was the GREATEST Electrical Inventor?

Dear Reader

Imagine arriving home to find that the power was not on. You wouldn't be able to switch on the lights, the TV, or your computer. Everything in the fridge would be warming up, and everything in the freezer would be slowly starting to thaw. If it was winter, you wouldn't be able to put on the electric heater.

WE SHOULD REMEMBER THE CLEVER PEOPLE IN THE PAST WHO INVENTED ELECTRICAL TECHNOLOGY.

When we think about this, it becomes very clear how important electricity is in our lives. We enjoy using our electrical appliances because clever people in the past invented electrical technology to make our lives easier today.

I hope you enjoy reading about some of the electrical inventors who have helped to make our lives easier!

Sharon Parsons

For learning solutions, visit **cengage.com.au**

Contents

Who Was the GREATEST Electrical Inventor?

1 Electricity as Energy

The **Energy** in **Water**

Electricity is a form of energy. Electricity results from the movement of tiny particles called electrons. When electrons move between atoms, the flow of energy is called electricity.

ELECTRICITY

The word "electricity" was first used in 1646 by an English scientist, Sir Thomas Browne.

Water Energy

It takes energy to make electrons move. There is a lot of energy in the force of running water, especially in rivers. The energy of moving water can be changed into electrical energy in three main ways:

- **Rivers: used in hydro-electric dams, which produce about 25% of the world's power.**
- **Tides: used in tidal power stations, which are less common.**
- **Waves: used in wave power stations, which are less common.**

Physical Science

Magnets and Generators

The energy of moving water is changed into electricity using magnets. The water's energy spins a magnet near a wire. The movement of the magnet, powered by the energy of moving water, makes electrons move between atoms in the wire. As a result, electricity flows along the wire. A machine like this that changes one form of energy into electricity is called a generator.

Case Study: A Hydro-Electric Dam

A hydro-electric dam uses the energy of a river to turn huge magnets in huge generators.

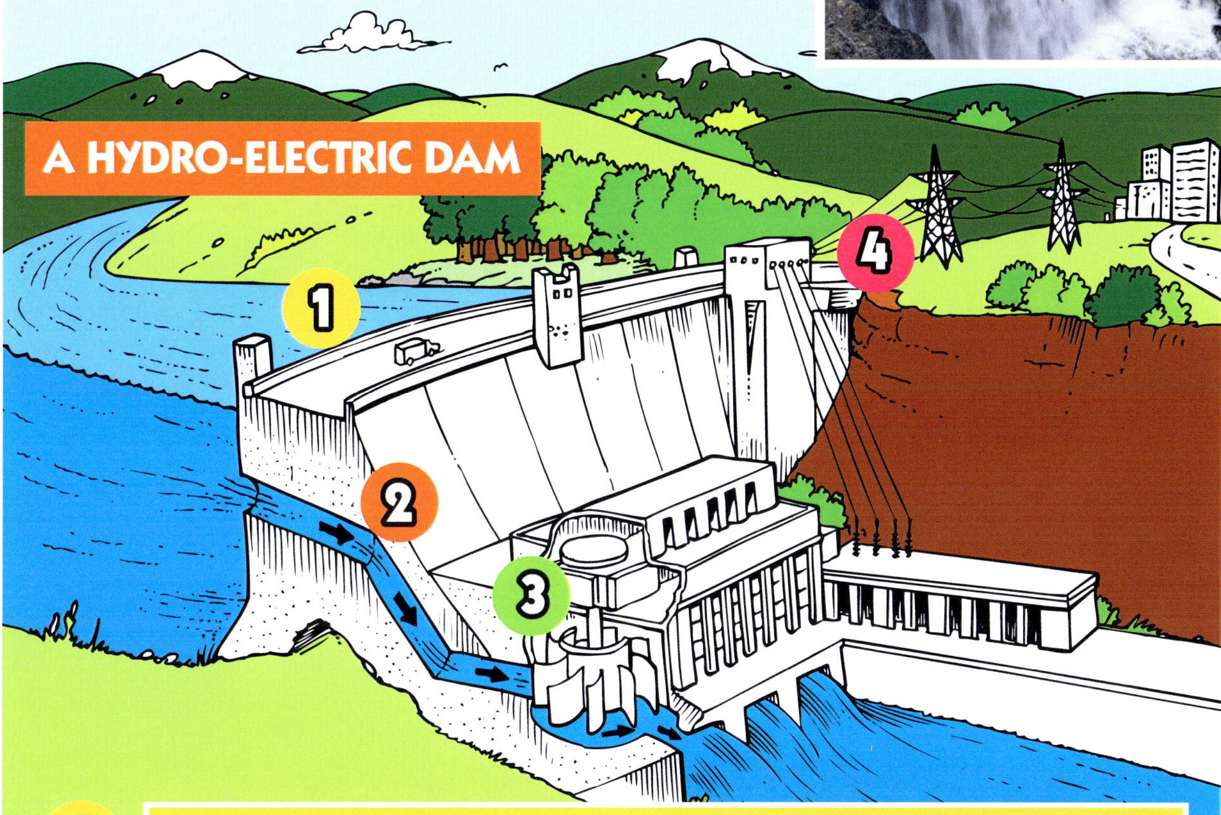

1. Water from the river is stored in the hydro-electric dam.
2. Water flows down through pipes and spins the blades of a machine called a turbine.
3. The turbine is connected to a generator. The spinning turbine moves a magnet in the generator, which produces electricity.
4. The electricity travels through electrical wires and transformers to homes, schools, transport facilities and many other places.

2 Renewable Energy Sources

Using the Energy in our **Environment**

a wind turbine

Wind, sunlight and moving water are forms of "renewable" energy. They can be reused and renewed, unlike coal or gas, which can only be used once. It is better for our environment to use more energy from renewable sources rather than non-renewable sources.

Wood is also a renewable energy source, because it can be grown over and over again – but this can take many years.

BIOMASS ENERGY

Energy from trees, or crops grown for fuel, is called biomass energy.

Wind Energy

Wind is moving air. The wind's energy is used to generate electricity through wind turbines. Wind energy is a fast-growing energy source for people around the world.

Solar Energy

The Sun produces heat energy and light energy. The Sun's energy is called solar power.

The Sun's energy can be changed into electricity using solar panels. Solar panels can be fitted to the roof of a house, where they can produce electricity to power lights and other electrical appliances.

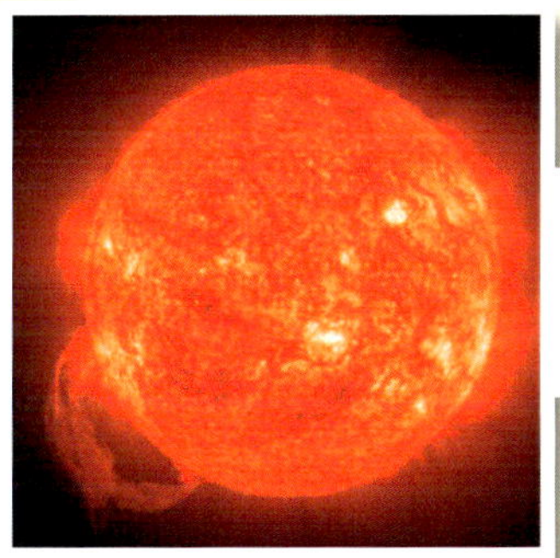

The Sun produces an enormous amount of energy.

solar panels

Physical Science

Sunlight and Solar Power

solar panels

Sunlight is made up of a stream of light particles called photons. When photons hit a solar panel, they carry their energy into it and give this energy to the electrons in the solar panels. The electrons move and produce electricity.

Non-Renewable Energy Sources

Energy for Light, **Heat** and Cooking

Non-renewable energy sources, such as oil, coal and gas, cannot be replaced once they have been used. Burning these resources produces greenhouse gases and can add to global warming and climate change.

coal storage

Before Power in Homes

Before electricity became available to homes in the early 1900s, people used the following energy sources.

Wood: a renewable energy source that is burned mainly for cooking and heating. But trees take many years to grow.

Oil: a non-renewable energy source that is burned mainly for cooking and heating.

Coal: a non-renewable energy source that is burned for cooking and heating. It can be burned to make steam for steam trains.

Gas: a non-renewable energy source made from coal or oil. It is burned for cooking and heating, and used in gas lamps.

Energy Sources Today

In some parts of the world, people still use these energy sources. But most people would prefer to use more renewable and fewer non-renewable energy sources.

Saving Electricity

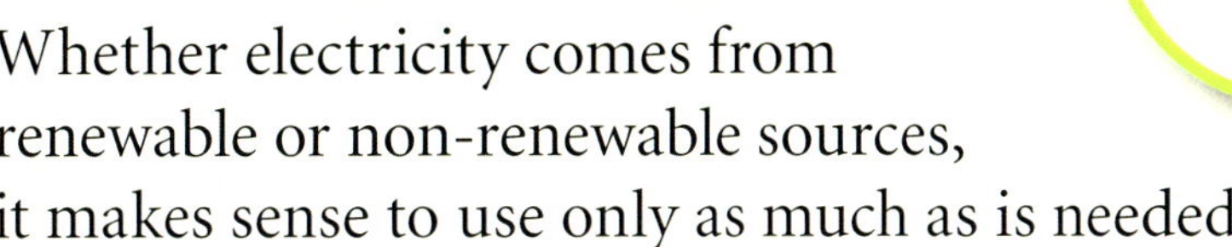

Whether electricity comes from renewable or non-renewable sources, it makes sense to use only as much as is needed.

Below are some ways to save electricity and conserve the resources used to make it.

1

New Products: only buy new products when they are needed. Factories and shops use electricity to make, transport and sell things. Recycling products and materials can save energy.

2

At Home: switch off lights and appliances, and have shorter showers. Install insulation so that less electricity is needed for heating and cooling. Use light globes and appliances that use less energy.

3

Switch Off: turn off TVs and computers at the wall to save electricity.

4

At School: turn off computers, lights and other electrical equipment when the classroom is not in use.

4 Great Electrical Explorers

Scientists

Scientists have worked hard to find ways to use electricity. No one invented or discovered electricity.

Early Electrical History

In 1600, an English scientist called **William Gilbert** published a famous book about magnets and magnetic fields. He was the first scientist to discover that Earth is magnetic. This helped people understand many things, such as why compass needles pointed north-south.

In the USA in the 1700s, inventor and scientist **Benjamin Franklin** studied electricity and showed that lightning was electrical.

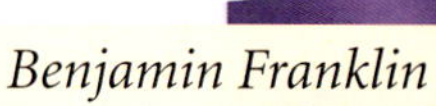

Benjamin Franklin

By 1800, scientist **Alessandro Volta** had made the first battery. The "volt", a unit measuring electric force, is named after him.

In 1821, scientist **Michael Faraday** invented the first electric motor, after much work with electricity and magnets.

The work of these and other scientists helped the electrical inventors featured in this book.

Inventors

In **Chapter 5**, you will meet three electrical inventors:

- Thomas Edison
- Nikola Tesla
- George Westinghouse.

In **Chapter 6**, you will meet four inventors who used electricity for their inventions:

- Josephine Cochrane
- Grace Hopper
- Hedy Lamarr
- Barbara Askins.

Nikola Tesla

Josephine Cochrane

Social Studies

Patents for Inventions

An inventor can apply for a patent to register their new invention. Inventors register their invention at a patent office. The patent protects their invention from others who may try to copy their idea and sell it for money.

5 Men of Electricity

Meet Thomas Edison

Thomas Edison was born in Ohio, USA, in 1847.

A Boy Invents at Home

As a child, Edison did not do well at school, so his mother taught him at home. She set up a laboratory for him where he did experiments and invented things.

Famous and Clever

Edison became a famous scientist and businessman. His inventions changed the way people lived and communicated.

Famous Electrical Inventions

First Long-Lasting Light Bulb

In 1880, Edison invented a light bulb that glowed when an electric current passed through it. Unlike earlier light globes, this one lasted a long time and was practical for use in homes.

First Power Plant

In 1882, the first power station, which had been built by Edison, started providing electricity to some homes in New York, USA. It provided the power needed to use Edison's long-lasting bulbs.

Other Edison Inventions

Phonograph

Edison's phonograph recorded sound on the tinfoil surface of a cylinder. It used a needle attached to a membrane. When sound vibrated the membrane, the needle cut tiny grooves in the tinfoil. The sounds could be replayed when a needle ran through the foil's groove as it turned around and around.

Movie Camera

Thomas Edison didn't invent the first movie camera. But he did invent the first one that was cheap enough for many people to buy.

Meet Nikola Tesla

Nikola Tesla

Nikola Tesla was born in 1856 in a village called Smiljan, in a country now known as Croatia.

A Boy with Ideas

When he was young, Tesla invented all kinds of things, but nothing that people could buy.

Tesla had a rare ability: he could "build" and "test" his inventions in his head. Tesla did not draw or write about his inventions.

Tesla and Edison

When Tesla moved to the USA he worked for Edison's company. Edison's electric motors and generators ran on direct current (DC), but Tesla wanted to change them to alternating current (AC), which sends energy one way and then the other way. Tesla thought AC would be much more efficient.

Tesla in his laboratory

Edison, however, had built his company using DC, so he did not want to replace his existing equipment. The two men disagreed so Tesla had to leave Edison's company.

Inventor Rivals

After Tesla left Edison's company, they became rivals. Imagine what they might have invented if they had continued to work together.

Tesla's Electric Light Company

Tesla started his own electric light company in 1886. He planned to use his ideas for AC but others in his company disagreed with his plans. Later that year, he was forced to leave. With no money, Tesla had to work as a road builder.

Tesla's AC Breakthrough

Tesla kept thinking about how to improve his AC motors and generators. In 1888, he was offered a job by George Westinghouse, at his electrical company.

a picture of Tesla, depicting him "sparking" with electricity

In 1892, Tesla's first inventions using AC electricity were patented, including early fluorescent lamps. In 1893, Westinghouse and Tesla lit up an international exhibition using AC power in Tesla's fluorescent lamps.

Today, AC is used everywhere to power homes, appliances, factories and many other things. Tesla is remembered for this, and his many other useful electrical inventions.

Technology

Tesla's Inventions

Tesla invented many things, including everyday objects like the car speedometer and the radio. One of his ideas helped others to invent the X-ray.

Meet George Westinghouse

George Westinghouse was born in New York, USA, in 1846.

George Westinghouse

A Lazy Boy

When he was a child, George's school teachers said he was lazy. It was this trait that helped him to become a very good inventor. When his father gave him work to do, the young Westinghouse would invent something to make the work easier.

Westinghouse and Steam

In 1865, Westinghouse invented a rotary steam engine. Steam engines were used a lot in those days, to power trains, factory equipment, ships and other machinery.

a steam engine

Tesla Joins Westinghouse

Westinghouse realised Tesla was a great inventor. Working together, the two men thought up electrical inventions that changed the way people live and work.

Westinghouse's Best Inventions

Westinghouse and his company invented many important inventions, but among his most famous are air brakes, transformers and extra big electric generators.

Air Brakes

Air brakes helped train drivers to stop quickly. Before air brakes, steam engines braked the whole train, or men in each carriage applied the brakes when the engineer blew a whistle. There were many train accidents because brakes weren't applied in time.

Transformers

Transformers are used to send electricity over long distances. This allows homes and businesses to have access to electricity, even if they are a long way from the power plant.

Extra Big Electric Generators

Westinghouse's company invented and built three huge electric generators. They used the energy from water falling over Niagara Falls to make electricity. This was a very early use of hydro-electricity.

Steam Engines

The trains on pages 16–17 are powered by steam. Steam forces a train's pistons to move in cylinders. The movement back and forth turns the wheels round and drives the train.

a steam engine

the Niagara Falls

6 Women of Electricity

Meet Josephine Cochrane

Josephine Cochrane invented the first mechanical dishwasher, which she showed publicly in 1893. She wanted a machine that would wash her china dishes faster and better than her servants could.

Josephine Cochrane

Dishwasher Design

Cochrane couldn't find a machine so she built one herself. She designed and made the wire compartments to fit her dishes. The compartments were put into a wheel. The wheel was put into a big copper boiler.

the first dishwasher

Dishwasher Motor

A motor turned the wheel as hot, soapy water squirted from the bottom of the copper boiler to clean the dishes.

Dishwasher Production

Cochrane set up a company to make the dishwashers. At first, only hotels and restaurants bought them. But by the 1950s, people were starting to buy dishwashers for their homes. Electricity made this job much easier!

a modern dishwasher

Meet Grace Hopper

Grace Hopper was one of the first software engineers. Hopper thought computer programs should be written more simply. She helped people understand early computers.

Hopper and an early computer

A New Computer Language

In the 1950s, Hopper developed a computer language called COBOL. It was the first of its kind and was the basis of all later digital computing.

Tests for Computers

Hopper also developed tests for computer systems to make sure they matched certain standards.

Grace Hopper at work

Technology

Debugging a Computer

an original computer "bug"

Rear Admiral Grace Hopper invented the term "debugging" to describe how she fixed problems with her computer. One day, Hopper came up with the idea when she had to remove a moth from her computer.

Meet Hedy Lamarr

Hedy Lamarr was a famous movie star in the 1940s. But she still found time to invent a way to help American torpedoes reach their targets!

Hedy Lamarr

Stop the Torpedoes

During World War II, radio-controlled torpedoes were in use. The problem was that the enemy could easily find the radio frequency being used by a torpedo and jam it. Jamming the frequency allowed the enemy to stop the torpedo from hitting its target. Lamarr and a friend called George Anheil designed a torpedo guidance system that used constantly changing frequencies. This stopped the enemy from finding a frequency and jamming it.

Helped Communications

Lamarr offered her invention to the US military. But they did not use it. However, Lamarr's work has been used in satellites and military communications since the 1960s. Her invention also helped other inventors to design technology for communication devices, such as fax machines, mobile phones and other wireless products.

Lamarr's work helped others to develop mobile phones.

Meet Barbara Askins

Barbara Askins

Barbara Askins was a chemist. She invented a way to develop better films for X-rays and photos.

In 1975, NASA asked Barbara to find ways to develop their images of Earth and space.

an astronaut in space above Earth

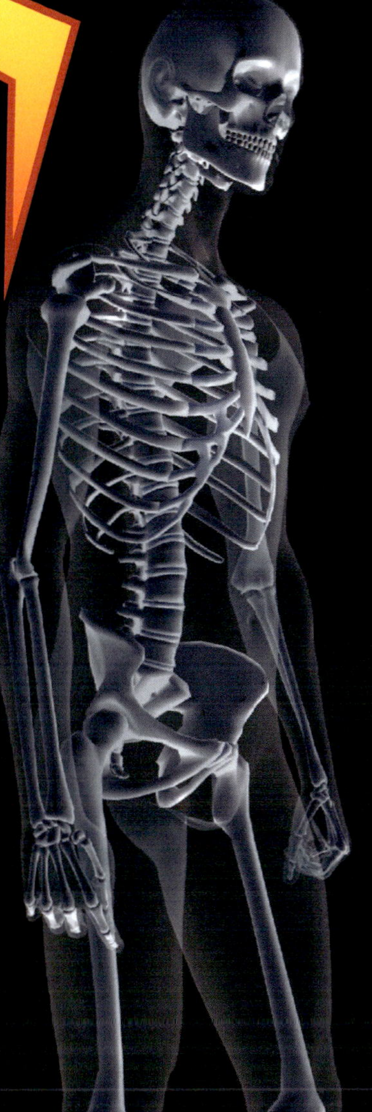
an X-ray image

Technology

X-Rays

Electricity in an X-ray machine sets electrons flying. They give off energy in the form of X-rays. These rays can penetrate bodies.

X-ray machines take "photographs" of the insides of a body. Hard things, like bone, appear white. Soft things, like muscle or organs, appear grey or black.

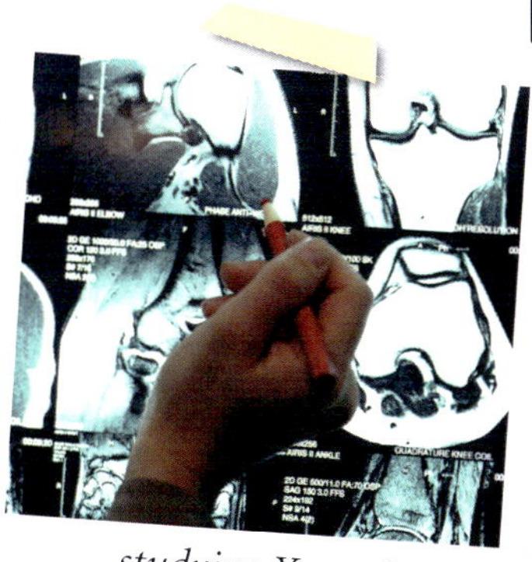
studying X-ray images

7 Help for the Hearing Impaired

A **Device** to Change Lives

The hearing aid helps people who are deaf or hearing impaired to hear more clearly. The first hearing aids were large, horn-shaped trumpets, used to collect sounds. These were known as "ear trumpets".

The modern hearing aid was designed by two great inventors – Thomas Edison and Alexander Graham Bell. Inventor of the telephone, Bell was able to amplify (or make louder) sound using a microphone and a battery. In 1886, Edison created a type of transmitter, which changed sounds into electrical signals that could travel through wires and be converted back into sounds. This technology was used in the first electrical hearing aids.

Large batteries made the hearing aids difficult to wear. In the 1950s the first transistor hearing aids were introduced. These were later adapted to fit behind the ear. In the 1990s the first digital hearing aid was made. These hearing aids had far greater sound quality and were easier to wear.

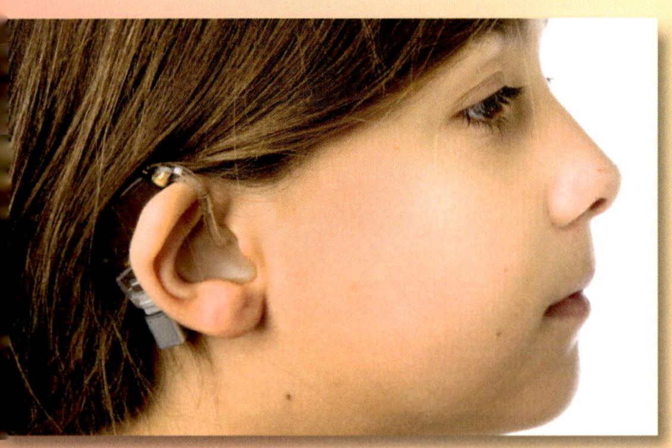

a girl wearing a modern digital hearing aid

Today, improvements in technology have helped to develop even smaller devices with excellent sound quality. They can be adjusted to suit the user and any change in environment, for example, from the quietness of the library to the loudness of a busy city street.

The hearing aid has come a very long way from the "ear trumpet" first created in the 1800s. It is an important aid used by people all around the world. Such an invention may never have happened without the incredible work of two great inventors – Alexander Graham Bell and Thomas Edison.

Alexander Graham Bell

Review and **Decide**

REVIEWERS

A reviewer's job is to write what they think about something that they have read, seen, heard or experienced.

Newspapers and magazines publish reviews, so that their readers can decide if they are interested in what is being reviewed. If you were a reviewer for a magazine called *Electrical Monthly*, which person would you nominate as the greatest electrical inventor?

Help for Your Review

A reviewer writing an article titled, "Who was the Greatest Electrical Inventor?", might ask the following questions:

Q. Which electrical inventor has helped us more in our homes?

Q. Which inventor invented more electrical inventions?

Q. Which electrical inventor do you think worked the hardest? Why?

Q. Which electrical invention do you like the most? Why?

Q. Which electrical inventor would you have liked to be?

You may need to reread parts of this book to help you write your review.

Index

Glossary

alternating current (AC)	A flow of electricity where the current is sent in one direction then the other (usually about 50 times per second)
atom	A building block of matter, made up of a nucleus in the centre surrounded by a cloud of electrons
direct current (DC)	A flow of electricity where the current is always sent in the same direction (for example, in a battery)
greenhouse gases	Gases, such as carbon dioxide and methane, which may form a blanket in the atmosphere that stops heat escaping from Earth
magnetic field	The area around a magnet where magnetic force may attract or repel other magnets and some metals
tidal power stations	Power stations that generate electricity by using the natural movement of water in ocean tides
turbine	A piece of machinery (in this case, in a power station) that spins around
wave power stations	Power stations that generate electricity by using the natural movement of water in ocean waves